WE ARE
SPECIAL

WRITTEN BY:

MARMAR STEWART

ILLUSTRATED BY:

NOOR STEWART

Dedicated to all children with
autism spectrum disorder
and to Noor and Ali Tiam,
for whom I would shake mountains.

All profits from this book
will be donated to the
speech therapy program at
Coralwood School, Decatur, Georgia.

Published by: Xanthus Design, Washington DC
ISBN: 978-0-9988836-0-1

It was a typical Tuesday night.

Caitlin was ready to go to sleep.
She had already put on her pajamas and
brushed her teeth, and she was now in bed.
Her mother was about to read her favorite
bedtime story.

All of a sudden, Caitlin asked,
"Mom, when will Travis learn to talk?"

"Sara's brother is just two years old,
and he can already talk."

"Mom, I can't wait to play with Travis and talk with him just like my friends play and talk with their little brothers. Sometimes he doesn't answer when I call his name, and he acts as if he doesn't see me."

Caitlin's mother sighed and said, "Honey, we hope Travis will be able to talk soon.

We just have to be patient and encouraging. Remember how we learned to talk to him by using pictures and words together?

Most children with autism have difficulties with communication, but with love, care, and practice, they can overcome these challenges. I promise you."

Caitlin's mother read her favorite bedtime story until she fell asleep.

The next day, Caitlin's mother came down
the stairs and saw Travis playing with his cars.
He had put them all in a row.

She sat next to Travis and started
playing with him. She practiced the colors
with him, saying softly but clearly,

"This is a yellow car." "This is a blue car."
"This is a green car." "This is a red car."

That afternoon, Caitlin's school bus arrived. Caitlin walked down the sidewalk from the bus stop talking with the other kids from her neighborhood.

When Caitlin arrived home, she said, "Hi Mom! Can I go to Angelina's house after I finish my homework?"

Caitlin's mother helped her hang up her backpack and answered, "No, honey. Today is Wednesday. It's just about time for Daddy to Skype us from overseas."

Caitlin's and Travis's father is in the army serving the country. They miss him very much. He usually Skypes with them every Wednesday at 4 o'clock in the afternoon.

Caitlin smiled and said, "Right, Mom! How could I forget? Today is Wednesday. I want to show Dad the new drawing I made for him in Mrs. Haas's art class."

Caitlin's mother replied, "That's wonderful! I'm sure your father will be thrilled to see it."

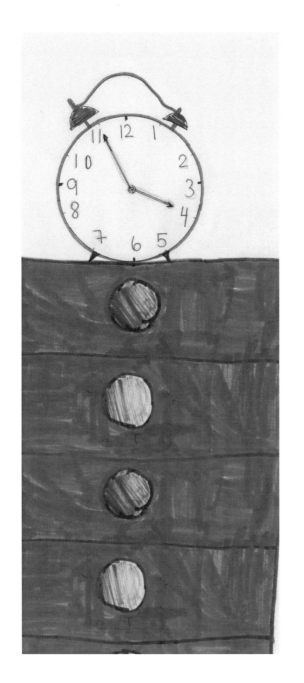

Shortly before 4 o'clock, they all sat together on the sofa. Travis got excited when his mother turned on the computer.

While they were waiting for the call, Travis played with the keys on the keyboard and watched the screen closely, and Caitlin got her drawing ready to show her father.

Caitlin and Travis were very happy to see their father appear on the computer screen.

After talking with him on Skype, they ate their dinner.
Caitlin and Travis played with his toy computer for a while
before brushing their teeth and getting ready for bed.
They both fell asleep with happy expressions on their faces.

A few days later, Caitlin's mother knocked on her door. She went in and saw Caitlin standing at her bedroom window, watching the kids from the neighborhood play in the street.

Caitlin's mother suggested, "Honey, if you're done with your homework, you can go outside and play with your friends."

Caitlin turned to her mother and said,
"Mom, I don't feel like playing outside today."

Caitlin's mother asked, "Honey, did something
happen at school? Is everything all right?"

Caitlin's mother knew her daughter very well.
She sensed that something was bothering
Caitlin. Caitlin's mother hugged her tight,
and they sat down together on Caitlin's bed.

Caitlin put her head on her mother's shoulder.

She asked, "Why is my brother different
from my friends' little brothers?"

Caitlin's mother put her arms around her and held
her tight. She said, "Caitlin, your brother Travis
is special, just like many other children out there."
"What do you mean, Mom?" asked Caitlin.
Her mother said, "We are very fortunate to learn
so many valuable lessons from Travis—lessons
like creativity, patience, acceptance, and
tolerance, just to name a few."

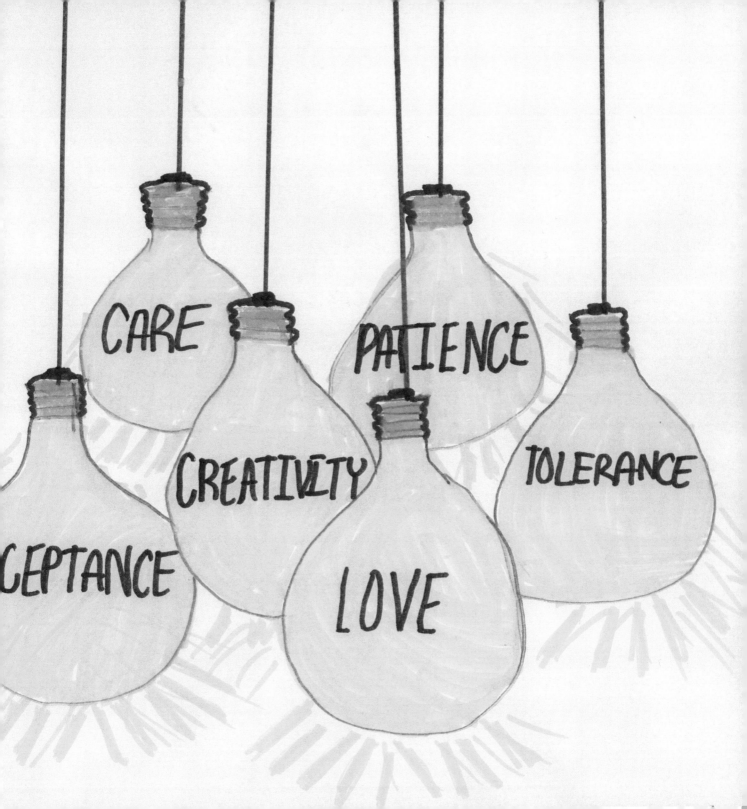

- "When we try to find ways to play and communicate with Travis, we learn to be creative."

- "When we face challenges and repeat tasks with love and care, we learn to be patient."

- "When we see the world through others' eyes, we become tolerant and accepting."

"Seeing the world through your brother's eyes
gives us more understanding of your brother
and of many people who are different from us.

Tolerance and acceptance make us better human beings. Just imagine—the world would be a much nicer place if everyone shared these experiences and had all these qualities."

"Do you see how fortunate we are? We are learning all these valuable lessons, and you are having this important experience at such a young age. I know sometimes it is not easy."

"You are a special sister because you are always very loving and understanding. You always do your best whenever you play with your brother Travis. You include him in everything that is fun for you. Remember how you helped him to decorate the Christmas tree or how you showed him the alphabet songs on the computer? Just think of all the other things you do with him."

"See what a special sister you are? See what a special brother you have? Just remember: it makes us special when we really think of others."

Caitlin smiled and agreed, "Yes, Mom! Travis is special, and we are special, too!"

The following Sunday, Caitlin was helping her mother clean up the playroom when she heard the doorbell ring.

"I'll get the door, children!" Caitlin's mother called. Caitlin was just about finished cleaning up the playroom. All of a sudden she heard Travis repeating,

"Daddy, Daddy, Daddy, Daddy ..."

Caitlin yelled, "Travis is talking! Mommy, listen! Travis is talking!" Caitlin was so overjoyed to hear Travis talking that she almost tripped over herself as she ran to the front room.

Her father had planned
a surprise for them and had just walked in the door.
He was hugging Travis, who was still repeating,
"Daddy, Daddy, Daddy."
When Caitlin's father saw her, he held
Travis tight with one arm and held out his other
arm for her. She ran to her father and Travis
and hugged them both.

Caitlin squeezed her father and Travis
and said joyfully,

"We are a special family.
We are all special together!"

THE END

Illustrated by Noor Stewart, age 10.
A fifth grader at Fernbank Elementary School.

Special thanks to Bardia Naziri
for the front cover and title page illustrations

www.WeAreSpecial.net
www.WeAreSpecial.info

This is a story of how one family's love, patience and caring brings richness to their lives as they work together to support a child with autism. We also learn how acknowledging and accepting difference can enrich us all. Told clearly and with delightful pictures, this is a perfect book for all families with young children whether or not they have "special" child.

Dr. Wendy Newby, M.Ed., Ph.D.

Beautifully written and illustrated, this book is an impressive, heartfelt treatment of a sensitive issue, elegantly conveying a message of hope, dedication, and support for the parents and siblings of children with autism spectrum disorder."

Dr. Naghi Momeni, Ph.D. *Specialist in Biomedical Sciences and Autism Research*

Marmar Stewart touches on a very important topic, the feelings of siblings of children with disabilities, in her book, We are Special. These siblings experience a rollercoaster of emotions that often are overlooked by overwhelmed parents. Siblings need attention, understanding, and reassurance too. Thank you, Marmar Stewart, for remembering these sometimes forgotten children.

Dr. Melanie Castelle, Ph.D. *Principal, Coralwood School*

Marmar Stewart is married and a mother of two. Born in Lorestan and raised in Hamburg, Germany, she now lives in Atlanta, Georgia. From a young age, she has been dedicated to taking steps for human rights and social issues. She is determined to play a role in raising awareness of autism and supporting efforts to improve its diagnosis and treatment.

$12.95

ISBN: 978-0-9988836-0-1
51295